good deed rain

This is the author's 56th book.
Others include: *Bowl of Water*,
The Mermaid Translation,
I Can Only Imagine, Magic Island,
The Orphanage of Abandoned Teenagers,
Something Bright,
and many more...

forest

and

field

FOREST & FIELD ©2022
Allen Frost, Good Deed Rain
Bellingham, Washington
ISBN 978-1-0880-5399-7

Writing & Drawings: Allen Frost
Cover Painting: Laura Smith
Cover Production: Priya Shalauta
Apple: TFK!
Drawings on 140/148 from *Another Life*

"After we got into the air we watched the birds. After we were taught by the air we could understand why birds did certain things during their flights. We learned why a bird suddenly drops and rises, and why the different positions of the bird when flying. In fact, we learned a great many things that we didn't know before."

—Wilbur Wright, *New York Globe*, May 30, 1912

FOREST & FIELD

Allen Frost

Good Deed Rain ◊ Bellingham, Washington ◊ 2022

INTRODUCTION

The future of this book is a shelf in a Goodwill. Someone will open it and check the penciled price and think about it. If they decide to buy this book, they will discover what it was like in the long-ago summer of 2022 while I was going from forest to field.

FEATURING

pretending

the

world

SEHOME HILL

I went to the top of Sehome Hill and sat on a rock and I heard a train of geese getting louder. Then I saw them in the leaves and they flew past at exactly my height. I picked up a marble snail and moved it off the trail. A weird bowery squirrel jittered and had a fit right in front of me. It looked possessed by something, so I took a different path. Watched a bumblebee an inch off the ground slowly come up to my shoe. Lots of birds singing. I passed a girl who might have been a robot. I went into Old Main to tear a scrap of paper off the bulletin board so I could write this down.

PRETENDING the WORLD

Birds sing in waves in the same way the breeze moves the flowers. The air is alive. Bees ring a rhododendron. There's an alligator flopped in the path. I'm pretending it isn't a broken log. I'm pretending the world in the woods on Sehome Hill is a dream. A junco comes to visit where I sit, whispers a secret and flies away.

DUCKS in the HORSE FIELD

We went to the horse field this morning. The woods smelled like rain, puddles were already starting on the path like fingerprints left by the creek. When we got to the horse field, we were in a gritty rain. I threw the ball for our dog and spotted ahead of us a pair of ducks. They see us too, long necks up like periscopes. They don't like this development. I get the feeling they've been together a while, a married couple who found this wet patch of ground when it was dawn and no one was around and now they're forced to leave. When the ball bounces towards them, and it becomes clear the dog is headed their way full speed, they takeoff loudly. Maybe they put a down payment on this plot, maybe they've been looking for a spot to raise a new family and they thought this was it.

Real estate isn't easy to find around here, even for a duck. They went over me low enough I could see into the eye of the wife as she looked down and scolded me. The husband was carrying their bags. The dog returned to me, dropping the ball, tail wagging, waiting for me the throw it again. The ducks made three more loops over me. Each time the wife gave me another choice curse. I apologized but she wanted more. She wants us to dig a pond filled with waterlilies and cattails on the edge, somewhere with dragonflies, and one single goldfish to tend the weeds that feed them.

1962 THUNDERBIRD

A hummingbird chases a crow. They veer right over me, low, the sunlight makes flashing red light on the hummingbird and I can't help thinking of those Hollywood car chases. I'll be glad when the car age is over. I won't miss their noise or how they stole our fresh air. Today someone parked a monument at the entrance to Sehome. A 1962 Thunderbird. People must have thought they were seeing a spaceship from another planet. It doesn't even have to move.

EVERY DIFFERENT SONG

On top of Sehome Hill, I sit at the controls of a radio station. Listen. To the east you can hear the steady current of traffic on I-5. Imagine the interstate is a mountain river. Then I turn that down and dial up the sound of birds. Every different song tells me what's going on.

The PORTLAND PARAKEET CLUB

When I lived in Portland, I went into a café that had a
new jukebox. They were all excited about it and asking
people to bring in records to stock it. The next day I
brought them the "Parakeet Training Record." The
girl at the counter was not enthused, in fact I don't
think it ever made it to the turntable, locked to the
spindle, with the sound of a dime falling in and the
crackling rush of a needle. That fate didn't even occur
to me—I was imagining the Portland Parakeet Club
that would soon form, meeting once a week, gathered
around the jukebox, everyone with a talkative little
bird wearing a mortarboard hat and a diploma tucked
underwing.

A NEW NEIGHBORHOOD

I know this path, I used to follow the dirt like a familiar sidewalk, but a month of rainy spring has tangled it and turned it to overgrowth, a thicket of branches and leaves. To my surprise I get lost in it. It's like a new neighborhood. There are green high-rises as tall as me, balconies, balustrades, restaurants and laundromats. I believe I hear the faint hoot of a train. It's true—as I push aside a glimmer of pink and yellow lanterns strung to a vine, I see a chain of beetles hauling a load of fiddleheads and spruce tips.

The RACCOON

A raccoon bundled in fur stops to check his pockets by the rainspout. He pulls out a watch on a chain, he knows he's late, it's nearly 8 AM. Who knows what errands kept him out all night? He puts his watch in his other hand and digs around until he finds a key. That's what he was looking for. The fir tree grown on the edge of Fairhaven Tower #6 has a door. He drops the key, mutters, brushed it off and went home.

BUTTERCUPS

Our street is quiet, no sound of bombs, no tanks or bullets, no screams, the birds around here are little puffs of life and I'm flat on the ground with the buttercups.

ANOTHER ANGEL

Another angel appears, it doesn't matter where, anywhere on Earth will do, they are welcome everywhere.

The SHUTTER

As I was walking past a tree, a bit of it fell off before me. Nothing so big as a branch or broad leaf, it was small, only an inch, and landed without a sound. I thought about it and turned around and went back to get it. Here it is in my hand. A tiny square of soft bark like a postage stamp. All mossy on one side, I search for a message on it, something a centipede might have written before it shut the window up there and realized the shutter had fallen off.

UNDERWATER

Today I will swim up Sehome Hill. I wear a wetsuit with flippers. The woods swirl in my facemask. A few strong motions and I'm in the ferns. Whatever I see today will be underwater. A dugong, an octopus, a school of fish that fly like birds from weed to weed.

The JAPANESE HOUSE

Japan? I can't say for sure where it's from. This might not even be a house. But it sure looks like one. Built in a hollow tree stump. Look at the roof, it's made of slanted ferns. It reminds me of a fairy tale where a badger lives in a teakettle in far-off Japan.

The RESERVOIR

I've been there so many times I can tell you exactly what's happening while I'm not there. I can describe the way the sunlight looks in the leaves around the reservoir, the sound of songbirds and a bee looking for flowers. But the water always changes, it depends on the sky and if a breeze is brushing the reflection.

The HORSE FIELD

I bet it's been fifty years since there's been a horse in this field. In 1972 you could see two of them from the road. Then for a couple years there was only one. It stood in the middle of the weeds near the apple tree. It would do that all day, rain or shine. When it was gone, the name stuck, it remains The Horse Field. The dog and I go there every day. This morning it was pouring rain. The exact moment I let our dog off leash, a rabbit hopped onto the path in front of us. What followed was exactly what you would expect.

CELLOPHANE

It's been a week since we saw the Cinderella play at the high school. Our son was in the orchestra. He still has the songs stuck in his head. He had to play them over and over for a month. They're still in the air. There's a tree tall enough to have a branch with a view of the school and I heard those songs fiddling up there, faint and fading, slow as cellophane with each passing day.

The DEER TRAIL

We stop to examine the deer trail, the dog smelling low to the ground, while I look at their flattened path, how it moves along the ridge of the hill, and the tall buttercups that must brush them as they walk through, painting them with yellow light.

A BEAUTIFUL DAY

First, realize you can fly. Steer in the air to your favorite branch with the best view in town, with the sun on you. A beautiful day. As it fills you up, you will find the words to say that all you want is right next to your heart. You can't help but tell how you feel, the way a prayer will fill a page and make a song of life.

SPOTLESS

The man in the blue shirt uniform is sweeping the cement. The broom coughs back and forth flicking leaves and catkins and fir needles until Sehome Lot 8G is spotless.

The SNAIL SHEPHERD

I have a second job, picking up snails. I didn't need to
apply or interview, and it has no set hours or pay. All
I have to do is watch where I'm going and make sure
I don't step on anyone.

A RABBIT BOOK

Sewn into the sunlit grass we see a rabbit standing up
and reading from a book. It knows we're near, but
it keeps a paw running along the page, the feel of
paper soft as cloth. We're right on the edge. If we take
another step closer, it will drop everything and run.

BELLINGHAM PUBLIC SCHOOL NO. 501

The bus comes to the field this morning, the last day of school. 41 kids have gone back and forth in it all year. For all they care the bus can sit out summer here, rust and be an orange flower.

The ICE CREAM BIRD

Somewhere hidden in the leaves, it mimics the calliope chimes of an ice cream truck, a haunted sound that makes you want to run to it, with a quarter held warm in the palm.

The PERFECT SPOT

I want to lie down in the sun, feel the pull of the undertow and let go, but the rabbit already beat me to the perfect spot, stretched out long like a stuffed pillow.

SUDDENLY

A cloud goes across the sun and suddenly the world
turns dark. The dog barks and stands up.

23 WORDS

A tiny red bug crawls over my knee. It's amazing that something so easily unseen could turn into the star of twenty-three words.

MY PET CROW

This bird isn't like the others. It flies on the ground like a shadow. I catch a glimpse of the black wings as it runs over the clover.

The OLD DOG

I used to see an old dog on the path. He couldn't walk, he rode in a child's red wagon. He was too old to shuffle anymore, but he was wrapped in thick tartan blankets and could still muster a bark if he needed to.

SKY-BLUE PLASTIC

Familiar, but every time I walk through here, I see something new. Today, it's a fly on a sky-blue scrap of plastic.

A WALRUS

I have never seen a walrus in the field. I'm sure the thought never crossed my mind before. Yesterday, it would have been a complete surprise to me if I saw one, but now I'm prepared…I feel like I'm just waiting to see a walrus.

OUR OWN FIELD

A baby deer in our backyard, not much bigger than
our dog, it wobbles, it wears white spots that bounce
in the dew and spill towards the blackberry, not in any
danger from us, safe in our own field.

The OPPOSITE

There's no newspaper vending machine or TV set in the field. I'm not here for their view of the world, difficult as it may be to get away from, it's my intention to notice the opposite of the news.

The FAKE FIELD

We went for a walk in the fake field, the land the factory left when it disappeared. Among the metal relics are broken bottles and cans, and the plants that grow bristle to the touch, rust-colored leaves that tick the breeze like clocks.

The FIRST TOURIST

Last week I saw the first swallow in town. Like any tourist, it was sightseeing. With a cup of coffee at a café, it wrote postcards to everyone it knew. By summer the word will spread and turn into shiny traffic veering above the field.

The RABBIT WATCHERS

They stand in the field, a big group of them, all ages, holding binoculars and cameras. The guide leads them closer to a thicket and that's where they spot their first rabbit. Ears poke above the weeds. The excitement flutters. Then someone points, "Look! There's another!"

WHEN I was a STATUE

There's a statue at the south end of the high school football field. It's me, holding a taut leash leading to a dog only two feet from a rabbit. A tense conversation is transmitted, silently, but there are scribbles between them. I'm stuck in time, waiting until they're done.

The CARTOON RABBIT

It happened long ago and all I'm really sure of is the cartoon rabbit. He wasn't like a friend I would want, he was someone you grew accustomed to on Saturday mornings in a room with blue carpeting when the sun was drumming on the window, waiting outside with the real world.

OUR BIRD

What does our bird wear, leaving the nest? A t-shirt of a favorite band and a pair of wings ready for the air.

The LUCKY MERMAID

That house on 50th Street where reckless waters
shook me, I held on best as I could to whatever there
was, like a limpet when the tide is rushing in. To know
those days is to blast open some subterranean tunnel
connected to the sea, then holding on tight as the
Pacific Ocean sweeps back and forth and pulls me
tumbling free. It's a lucky thing a mermaid appeared.

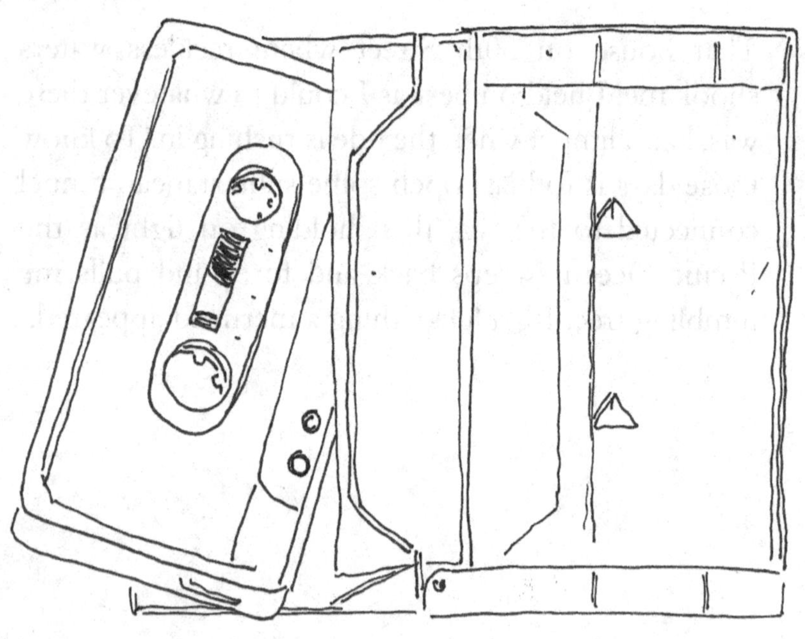

PART of the SOUNDTRACK

Back in my courting days, it's hard to believe the Smothers Brothers were part of the soundtrack, singing "I Talk to the Trees." Don't worry, there was also Los Indios Tabajaras, Gabby Pahinui and Coltrane, Hungarian violins, records and cassettes on the floor. Everyone should have that pleasure, warm with someone you love, serenaded by the stereo. The Garden of Eden is real, I can remember what it was like.

FIELD RECORDINGS

I made a cassette of a story and a play. There's no way now to know what they were, I just remember carrying the tape machine up the hill as I recorded. I wanted my voice to be mixed in with the background interstate trucks and cars. Time-travel to a field in Avalon, Mississippi in 1928.

The SOUND on the MOON

On the moon you wouldn't expect to hear much, but there was a movie I watched late one night after work. Astronauts were walking around on the moon. The set was what you'd expect from a movie like that, but the thing that caught my attention was the sound on the moon. I didn't know they had birds on the moon, singing as the earth rises in the black sky. It's after 1 AM, time to go to bed, I guess. I keep the window open so the real birds will wake me in the morning.

EELGRASS

In the Meadows River, the sound of an outboard motor. The boat carves through the channels, little islands, some no more than shoals, poke from the water. Coming up is Marsh Monkey Island. They chatter in the pine and look how they like to swing and throw mussel shells. The shallows are a field of eelgrass. The motor stops. The hush as the hull rushes over the weeds and skates up the stones onto land.

The GREEN GRASS OCEAN

I made a splash in the horse field. All the tall grass
turned into waves radiating away from me. Then,
when I hold myself still, the breeze dies down, the
calm returns.

The COBBLER

Anytime I see a millipede crossing the path, I think about those puttering feet. What's the rush, what's so important over there? I follow and find out. A cobbler shop where they can repair shoe number 102.

TELL the DRAGONFLIES

For the moment the field is for sale. There's a number to call. Fortunately, the International United Field Buyers comes to the rescue. They want to keep it for the future. You can tell the dragonflies not to worry.

BORAGE

Anyone can find a field. Look around. Yesterday I took a shortcut across a parking lot downtown and right there at my feet is the smallest green leaf growing in the crack of cement. I looked around and I could see more of them cautiously appearing. It shouldn't be a surprise to know there's a field growing right below. A borage stalk holds its head up like a flag.

STRANGE ANIMALS

I have spent a week away from work, but I got near to it with the dog yesterday. It felt like all I had to do was move a little closer into the woods that would be eerily lit and soon overgrown with strange animals and thorns on vines that would entangle me and pull me back into an office built from the grainy crooked timbers of Grimm's Fairy Tales.

A BLACK FOREST STORY

Her bright red coat really shows in the woods. When the sun in the leaves hits it just right, it makes her dapple. The birds have stopped singing, there's a wolf nearby.

HALO

Yes, I needed some rest. I'm back in the woods and everything is better. The bird opera. I can see distant hills and trees that reach to Canada. A cool breeze. When I walk the trail back to the office, I will take all this with me and let it spin around me like a halo.

A FAVORITE PLACE

Rabbits have their favorite places. This one sits between two parked cars and watches me go to work every morning.

ANGELS

They're people who can rise above the world we're in. They don't have wings, they don't need them. We are in awe of their ability.

The BIRD TRIBUNE

I've decided to make birdhouses. I'm going to fill the trees in the backyard, enough for everyone. I will post a notice in *The Bird Tribune* and wait for them to arrive.

KITTY HAWK

She looked at the ceiling in the office and asked me, "Are those fans new?" I told her no, they've been here for years, the Wright Brothers installed them, that's how old they are. Taken from the wings of their flying machine after it crashed in Kitty Hawk.

The SECRET MOUSE

He's turning circles like a wind-up toy. I catch him in a soup bowl and carry him to the backyard. This is the second one I've caught this way. Some nights we can hear them gnawing in the walls and running free, back and forth like the piano keys in a speakeasy.

TEA from the FOOT of MT. FUJI

A wooden boat, a sail calendar moved by the wind or not at all, wave after wave until time dissolves and when the mountain rises from the sea, it turns the hot water green.

The SAME THING SOMEWHERE ELSE

I can be in these trees and I remember other lives. The woods are full of them. I spent three minutes watching a bird go from branch to branch. I looked away for a moment and it was gone. I have to assume it's doing the same thing somewhere else.

The FIRST ROADS

They cut down the trees on Sehome Hill. The wood
was turned into the town below. Then they put a road
right over the top, with a tunnel through the limestone
peak, big enough for the tin cars of the time.

BEULAH LINDBERG

The Mount Baker memorial is a pyramid of stones clacked together. The penny-colored sign on it tells the names of the six people who got lost on that mountain on July 22, 1939. It helps to know their names, so you can picture them. Beulah Lindberg got up that sunny morning and gathered her ropes and stood on the corner waiting for her ride. We don't know what happened to these people, we only know they never came back.

INEVITABLE

Walking home, I passed by myself arriving for work. We didn't say anything. We both knew this was inevitable.

I KNOW a DINOSAUR

Now he'd give anything to be what he was, or even something different, like a bird waking up every morning singing.

The MOTH ARRIVES

I let the moth back into the office. It had been waiting on the door. Its wings were crisp from spending all night crowding around a ceiling lightbulb. It tumbled ahead of me, charting somewhere to land.

YARN

Sehome Hill is steeper today. Whoever lives beneath the ferns and trees has turned in their sleep like someone under a blanket. I'm climbing an arm up to a shoulder along the yarn of this breathing forest.

COWS

It came as a great surprise when it was discovered that cows can fly. We put a man on the moon, but they can jump a cow over it.

ECOLOGY

The horse field falls asleep and dreams that it drifts out to sea. It floats on stars, far enough from shore to be a new island with its own language and customs and ecology.

WONDERLAND

I still have dreamlike memory of seeing gondolas over Seattle. It's been my wish for a long time that there will be a string of them going up and down Sehome Hill. Imagine the views of the trees and rooftops and the bay. Windmills turn on the water's edge. We're up where the ravens see the world. Out the window, the other way, you can see the distant snowcapped mountains. Why can't the future be a wonderland? If we can picture it, it's real somewhere.

SWAINSON'S THRUSH

The song hops up a ladder and springs open wings on
the roof like an aerial. The bird repeats this until you
fade from hearing range.

UNCLE JOE

Today we are hiking on Chuckanut Hill. He finally
tells us his trouble. Being taller than everyone means
breaking all the spiderwebs strung in the path.

The JOB RECOMMENDATION

A girl at Old Main held the door open for me and I said, "Thanks. You should work at the Hilton."

The ORANGE

At 3 o'clock today I'll be eating an orange. That's the big news in the office today. A *Herald* reporter will be calling me at ten past the hour to get my reaction. That's the way it was supposed to go. But, driven by a hunch, the reporter called my office at 2:15 and when she got no reply, she hurried over. She found me holding a wet napkin filled with orange peels.

MORE than a CAR

An orange cat stands in the middle of the road watching me. I get closer, its tail goes clockwork. I tell it to get out of the road and sure enough a car appears. The cat is surprised, jumps, turns low and finds the curb in a hurry. This is how a tiger would look in someone's driveway. I can't resist stopping and call the cat over. Just like a tiger, it's wary. Funny, now it decides to look both ways for danger. I guess I'm more than 40 miles per hour and wheels. I scratch its neck and around its ear before I leave.

The GIFT of LIFE

An ember kept burning all the time spent running from danger and then settling warm, into those moments where it can lie down in the grass in the sun when it feels like heaven.

The JUNGLE COILS

The jungle would open into a clearing and part of the lawn would turn into quicksand. We would take turns falling in. Sometimes a garden hose could be a vine for rescue, to climb hand over hand, or in another second, just when you thought you were safe, it would change into a snake and catch you in coils.

SAINT JOSEPH'S MEDICAL CENTER

Walk in a maze of halls and rooms with doors left open to stories and agonies overheard in seconds like the old man who tells his wife, "I won't leave you," or the maniac in the emergency room who yells at the nurse to come home with him tonight and she replies, "That's not going to happen."

SNAIL

So I go back and forth all day, back and forth drawing
lines on the ground the way a snail will do when it
runs on worries and I grow accustomed to the rocks
and lilies on the path.

ABRAHAM

There's a young rabbit in our front yard who has the
face of Abraham Lincoln.

A PAIL of EELS

They bump together, thin as weeds, almost translucent,
holding onto each other like subway riders undersea.

RAIN STATION

We didn't go far in the woods today. It was starting to rain and I could tell by the tapping on the leaves, more little wet shoes were gathering, more rain was arriving like a crowd at a train station.

4:33 A.M.

Thelan Monday is taking the train, a woman is singing, an opera voice, as he joins the crowd going west. This is a dream, I know it as I am in it.

TILTED

A hundred years ago, a circus was camped near the field. Caravans filled with animals, show people, roustabouts. After a long tilted night, silhouettes and bonfires, in the early morning a clown sat on a folding chair and fished an oily puddle.

The LILIES of the FIELD

There are no lilies of the field, only the hard-won
daisies sewn into the yellow weeds. They hold on tight
in the wind. All they ever do is toil and spin.

The BUMBLEBEE

Every morning she crossed Fielding Avenue on her way to the Wendy's to work. She had a funny way of humming when she took someone's order. Hamburger, fries, soft drink, would set her off like a bumblebee.

MY OWN FOREST

There was an old ad that ran in the pulp comics that I couldn't resist. For $2.95, I could have my own forest. What I got for my money was a packet of seeds. If I could plant it, take care of it, give it water and shelter, it would become something to behold. A forest is only relative to your perception.

YOKO

It's true, my son was right. Today, "We heard a construction site that sounded just like Yoko Ono." On 13th and Mill Avenue, she is building spires taller than the telephone poles.

BUG TOW YARD

So this is where they come, crashed ants that have been stepped on, crumpled centipedes, dented ladybugs, balled-up spiders and flies that can't fly. The man in overalls will show you around but this isn't a place to dally, new wrecks are arriving all the time.

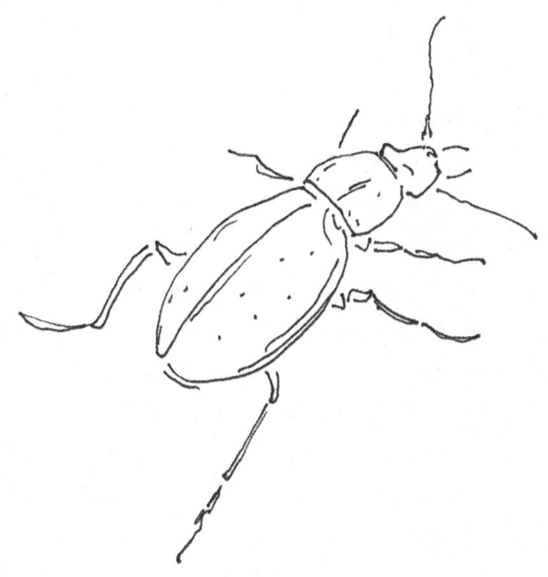

The FORTUNE TELLER

Your palm is soft, warm, the lines go from here to there. If we all knew exactly what would happen, we wouldn't need words.

The BROKEN BIRD

It repeats the same song on our fence, over and over like listening to an old friend tell a story you've heard again and again. You know where it's going, you know what will be said, but there's something so calming about it that time itself has been lulled and circles around it like a clock.

The FENCE

At least twice someone drove their car in the horse field, turning circles, tearing up the grass. You can still see the tracks. They still haven't mended. So this spring a silver chain-link fence was erected along Douglas Avenue. The last time I went through the gate I left it open, just wide enough for the deer to get through.

The LIONS CLUB

After my wife's car accident, we found out the local Lions Club will loan walkers, crutches, and wheelchairs if you have trouble walking. If you have trouble with lions, you can go to Maplewood Avenue, to the Club Club. Take your pick. Either aluminum or pine will do the trick.

HUNGRY

I bought $4 worth of bananas. The cashier asked if I wanted a receipt and I said, "No thanks, I've got a hungry gorilla waiting at home." People we meet momentarily leave us with mysteries.

12, 21

A quarter century ago when we moved to this northern mill-town, our TV got two stations: the local channel 12, and 21 was the Canadian Broadcasting Corporation. My favorite show on KVOS was hosted by the owner of the movie theater, and his college instructor friend. They sat in old easy chairs and discussed film classics. "Algiers" was one. Another time it was Val Lewton. On the CBC, my favorite program was about a disillusioned, lonely kid who could take a cottonball from his coat pocket and make a lady named Fluffy appear. She would sing and dance and bring joy to the world.

HAPPY BIRTHDAY

A 7-Eleven manager in Yonkers opens a pocketwatch
filled with sand and birds and rare butterflies and a
flying fish that sings your praise in Lebanese.

A DECORATED MIND

My uncle had a 1930s Royal Air Force Tiger Moth. He knew I liked planes and he offered to take me up in it. But I could foresee there would be barrel rolls and loops and the very good chance that some rivet or wire may come loose and we would plummet down, looking for a field to land. I'd be sitting behind the dead propeller as the wing would slash against the stalks of corn until we crumpled in. I declined. No heroics, no decoration. A ten-year-old victim of his own imagination.

The FREE RIDE

A swing has appeared in the woods. It's been carved and polished, and white ropes suspend it like jewelry from a cedar. How long can you resist? We are startled by a girl with long legs, laughing. The world is changed, this place has become a carnival in the trees, the swing is daring you to step right up and take a free ride. Right away you will remember something you left behind in third grade.

FEATHERS

Our neighbor came over with flowers. He and Diane heard about the car crash and wanted to check in. I told him how we are doing, and he said the other day he saw a hawk catch a mouse near here. It sat on the fence not ten feet away. He spoke to it the same way he does with the hummingbirds and then it took off and flew right past him. He could have touched the shining feathers.

CRADLE

At the doctor's office again, a woman checks in for her husband. He's got vertigo, he's waiting over there against the wall. When he walks towards us, bent over, slow as a heron, he cradles his too heavy head in his hands.

The PERFECT DAY in PARIS

Today we met Jules Verne, or should I say the reincarnation, Fern Julliard. She remembers *Twenty Thousand Leagues Under the Sea* and the creatures of *Mysterious Island*. She can remember the perfect day in Paris in 1859.

The PRESIDENT'S TWIN

He lives down Garden Street. I suppose he's like anyone else. Ordinary. He forgot to pay the telephone bill this month.

The DOLLAR TREE

Sometimes I'll push into the thicket to look for it. The money flutters on its branches. Can you imagine what would happen if people knew it was here? The war and greed that starts by just picking one little leaf.

The ROBOT'S VOICE

Every office day starts when I dial the robot for permission to work. I was used to her voice. She was familiar and forgiving, almost warm, almost human. There was a lilt when she said, "Bye," as if she knew we are all only temporary, even robots can be replaced.

HOVERED in the AIR

Is there a ghost of Jack Spicer at Aquatic Park? During baseball season he would be there every weekend with his transistor radio. The weather didn't matter. The Giants are playing at Candlestick Park, the seagulls are circling, spun around a crackle of poetry hovered in the air.

SEVENTH FLOOR

Next to a fir tree is a small gravestone: "Here Lies Birdy, Wilson's Warbler & Friend." I've buried my share of rabbits and birds and our family dog. Why do we do that, with a flower on top? We hope that space in the ground will lead like an elevator to another, even better place, where there won't be the worries of this world. And when it's your turn, you can see that little yellow warbler again, just listen for: "Seventh Floor… sunshine, running stream, warm breeze, Birdy."

The TOWER

Funny, I don't think I mentioned the tower on top of Sehome Hill. It's hard to miss. They sell postcards of it in shops. Our very own replica of the monument in Paris, a thousand feet of buttoned steel blinking with lights. At night it makes its own stars. It's a gigantic antenna where all our thoughts, phonecalls, radio and television signals, are flung to the far corners of the world.

PILLOWS

There are sheep in the field this morning—hundreds of them, I guess—from one side to the other. And they're all asleep. It's early, only 7 o'clock, we're the first ones here, and we've walked into a dream. The dew shines on the sunlit wool. If I let the dog go, she'll run across the tops of them like pillows.

The PINEAPPLE

A pineapple sits in our living room. It looks like a citizen of Mars who has come here sightseeing. We welcome it, we have made it the center of attention. We've been needing this exact distraction. It's hard to even notice you've been worrying.

EXPECTING a MIRACLE

A jar of blackberry jam is waiting for toast…It will be ready soon…The eager crowd has been growing since morning began and now they are fully surrounding the toaster with the hum of 20,000 people expecting a miracle.

DONALD MEEK

Those old movies are dreams in the shadows, all those actors and actresses, directors, and crews. Times change. They get out for a walk when they can. I saw Donald Meek in a gray suit and fedora. He held a 1946 nickel and he was looking for a good cup of coffee.

The CAPYBARA

A bit before midnight I got up and looked out the window and saw a strange animal on the grass, near the curb. It was tense as if sniffing the air. It was too small to be a deer, but not a dog, the shape was wrong. I guessed it might be a capybara. I don't know how one drifted so far north on a hot July night. The thermal conditions must have been just right. It stayed an animal for eight more seconds then I realized it wasn't. On 32nd Street in that very spot is a fire hydrant, so tame we almost forget it is there.

PITCH for an OSTRICH FARM

There are advantages, that much is obvious, the eggs are colossal, also if you want to eat an ostrich, it's like a 300-pound chicken. And weren't they once fashionable, didn't people wear ostrich feathers in their hats, or make elegant blue and silver robes from them, waving from the windows of zeppelins? It's all in a day. You can hitch your ostrich to a carriage, bring along a friend. Ride into town, sell your products at the market, and be back by sundown.

The BLACKBERRY CASTLE

Only a rabbit can get through the defenses. A low tunnel is chewed into the thorns, over the bits of a broken ladder that crashed and tangled long ago. Moving on, winding through the rusted cone of a bucket someone filled with berries and dropped by accident. Birds will find a notch between thorns and become radios. Twenty feet into the blackberry castle, there's a clearing. In the middle, a steamer trunk stands on end. Only the rabbit can see Sleeping Beauty projected in the beveled glass window. While she sleeps, she makes the pink flowers turn, green, then ripen into fruit. In another month blackberries will cover the castle walls.

GOOD MORNING

I was taught a new language in my dream, letters were written on the blackboard, a record was playing words for me to repeat. As soon as I had it right, I woke up.

LIKE MOST of MODERN AMERICA

"My clematis is crawling across the laundry line," she said. There's no more need for sun-warmed clothes in the breeze. Like most of modern America, we use a washing machine and a dryer. When we go outside, we have to duck the purple flowers.

WE WHO RIDE SWINGS

This isn't easy to report, but it happened, we turned the corner in the woods and the swing was gone. The ropes were cut and left hanging from the cedar branch. All you need to do is look at the news, it's been going on for years. This sort of thing seems to be happening everywhere these days. We kept walking. I was troubled, thinking about the swing, what it means, but the dog was smiling, happy to be leading me to the field where she would be jumping and catching and running. Whoever did that to the swing has no idea that we who ride swings happen to carry the feeling wherever we go—we know a joy that sends us through the air, from the past, through the present, into the future.

The SEHOME MARINERS

I could get lost in the undergrowth, I could sink deep
into the leafy waves. I could listen below to the burr
of a hummingbird and bees patrolling the flowers,
with me in slow-motion reaching for a salmonberry.

DELICIOUS

Today I picked my first blackberry on the corner of
32nd and Taylor Avenue. I was surprised they have
already formed on the vine, it seems early. It must be
the rush of cars, that hurried them to grow delicious.

TO BE BEAUTIFUL

Imagine the nerve it takes to be a deer in this town. To wake up somewhere hidden each day, then to be obvious and also to melt in, to be prey, to be beautiful and almost innocent, with a spotted baby to care for, crossing roads to look for something that doesn't seem to exist, getting used to grief, to cling to the idea of a peace that doesn't seem to exist except in the pure joy of sunlight and shade in the leaves, and the miracle of finding flowers in a garden someone forgot to cover with a fence.

PACIFIC WRENS

They go up and down the branch and call to me like distant rusty wheels. So small I could put all three of them in my shirt pocket and walk down the hill like a saint, spreading the music of a faint memory. Remember 1962, when Elvis rode the monorail on the blue night skyline above the streets of the World's Fair and sang a Seattle lullaby.

FOREST & FIELD
Writing:
May—August 2022

Illustration from *Another Life* (2007)

Books by Good Deed Rain

Saint Lemonade, Allen Frost, 2014. Two novels illustrated by the author in the manner of the old Big Little Books.

Playground, Allen Frost, 2014. Poems collected from seven years of chapbooks.

Roosevelt, Allen Frost, 2015. A Pacific Northwest novel set in July, 1942, when a boy and a girl search for a missing elephant. Illustrated throughout by Fred Sodt.

5 Novels, Allen Frost, 2015. Novels written over five years, featuring circus giants, clockwork animals, detectives and time travelers.

The Sylvan Moore Show, Allen Frost, 2015. A short story omnibus of 193 stories written over 30 years.

Town in a Cloud, Allen Frost, 2015. A three-part book of poetry, written during the Bellingham rainy seasons of fall, winter, and spring.

A Flutter of Birds Passing Through Heaven: A Tribute to Robert Sund, 2016. Edited by Allen Frost and Paul Piper. The story of a legendary Ish River poet & artist.

At the Edge of America, Allen Frost, 2016. Two novels in one book blend time travel in a mythical poetic America.

Lake Erie Submarine, Allen Frost, 2016. A two week vacation in Ohio inspired these poems, illustrated by the author.

and Light, Paul Piper, 2016. Poetry written over three years. Illustrated with watercolors by Penny Piper.

The Book of Ticks, Allen Frost, 2017. A giant collection of 8 mysterious adventures featuring Phil Ticks. Illustrated throughout by Aaron Gunderson.

I Can Only Imagine, Allen Frost, 2017. Five adventures of love and heartbreak dreamed in an imaginary world. Cover & color illustrations by Annabelle Barrett.

The Orphanage of Abandoned Teenagers, Allen Frost, 2017. A fictional guide for teens and their parents. Illustrated by the author.

In the Valley of Mystic Light: An Oral History of the Skagit Valley Arts Scene, 2017. A comprehensive illustrated tribute. Edited by Claire Swedberg & Rita Hupy.

Different Planet, Allen Frost, 2017. Four science fiction adventures: reincarnation, robots, talking animals, outer space and clones. Illustrated by Laura Vasyutynska.

Go with the Flow: A Tribute to Clyde Sanborn, 2018. Edited by Allen Frost. The life and art of a timeless river poet. In beautiful living color!

Homeless Sutra, Allen Frost, 2018. Four stories: Sylvan Moore, a flying monk, a water salesman, and a guardian rabbit.

The Lake Walker, Allen Frost 2018. A little novel set in black and white like one of those old European movies about death and life.

A Hundred Dreams Ago, Allen Frost, 2018. A winter book of poetry and prose. Illustrated by Aaron Gunderson.

Almost Animals, Allen Frost, 2018. A collection of linked stories, thinking about what makes us animals.

The Robotic Age, Allen Frost, 2018. A vaudeville magician and his faithful robot track down ghosts. Illustrated throughout by Aaron Gunderson.

Kennedy, Allen Frost, 2018. This sequel to *Roosevelt* is a coming-of-age fable set during two weeks in 1962 in a mythical Kennedyland. Illustrated throughout by Fred Sodt.

Fable, Allen Frost, 2018. There's something going on in this country and I can best relate it in fable: the parable of the rabbits, a bedtime story, and the diary of our trip to Ohio.

Elbows & Knees: Essays & Plays, Allen Frost, 2018. A thrilling collection of writing about some of my favorite subjects, from B-movies to Brautigan.

The Last Paper Stars, Allen Frost 2019. A trip back in time to the 20 year old mind of Frankenstein, and two other worlds of the future.

Walt Amherst is Awake, Allen Frost, 2019. The dreamlife of an office worker. Illustrated throughout by Aaron Gunderson.

When You Smile You Let in Light, Allen Frost, 2019. An atomic love story written by a 23 year old.

Pinocchio in America, Allen Frost, 2019. After 82 years buried underground, Pinocchio returns to life behind a car repair shop in America.

Taking Her Sides on Immortality, Robert Huff, 2019. The long awaited poetry collection from a local, nationally renowned master of words.

Florida, Allen Frost, 2019. Three days in Florida turned into a book of sunshine inspired stories.

Blue Anthem Wailing, Allen Frost, 2019. My first novel written in college is an apocalyptic, Old Testament race through American shadows while Amelia Earhart flies overhead.

The Welfare Office, Allen Frost, 2019. The animals go in and out of the office, leaving these stories as footprints.

Island Air, Allen Frost, 2019. A detective novel featuring haiku, a lost library book and streetsongs.

Imaginary Someone, Allen Frost, 2020. A fictional memoir featuring 45 years of inspirations and obstacles in the life of a writer.

Violet of the Silent Movies, Allen Frost, 2020. A collection of starry-eyed short story poems, illustrated by the author.

The Tin Can Telephone, Allen Frost, 2020. A childhood memory novel set in 1975 Seattle, illustrated by author.

Heaven Crayon, Allen Frost, 2020. How the author's first book *Ohio Trio* would look if printed as a Big Little Book. Illustrated by the author.

Old Salt, Allen Frost, 2020. Authors of a fake novel get chased by tigers. Illustrations by the author.

A Field of Cabbages, Allen Frost, 2020. The sequel to *The Robotic Age* finds our heroes in a race against time to save Sunny Jim's ghost. Illustrated by Aaron Gunderson.

River Road, Allen Frost, 2020. A paperboy delivers the news to a ghost town. Illustrated by the author.

The Puttering Marvel, Allen Frost, 2021. Eleven short stories with illustrations by the author.

Something Bright, Allen Frost, 2021. 106 short story poems walking with you from winter into spring. Illustrated by the author.

The Trillium Witch, Allen Frost, 2021. A detective novel about witches in the Pacific Northwest rain. Illustrated by the author.

Cosmonaut, Allen Frost, 2021. Yuri Gagarin's rocket lands in America. Midnight jazz, folk music, mystery and sorcery. Illustrated by the author.

Thriftstore Madonna, Allen Frost, 2021. 124 summer story poems. Illustrated by the author.

Half a Giraffe, Allen Frost, 2021. A magical novel about a counterfeiter and his unusual, beloved pet. Illustrated by the author.

Lexington Brown & The Pond Projector, Allen Frost, 2022. An underwater invention takes three friends through time. Illustrated by Aaron Gunderson.

The Robert Huck Museum, Allen Frost, 2022. The artist's life story told in photographs, woodcuts, paintings, prints and drawings.

Mrs. Magnusson & Friends, Allen Frost, 2022. A collection of 13 stories featuring mystery and ginkgo leaves.

Magic Island, Allen Frost, 2022. There's a memory machine in this magical novel that takes us to college.

A Red Leaf Boat, Allen Frost, 2022. Inspired by Japan, this book of 142 poems is the result of walking in autumn.

Forest & Field, Allen Frost, 2022. 117 forest and field recordings made during the summer months, ending with a lullaby.